Dear Parent:
Your child's love of reading starts here!

Every child learns to read in a different way and at his or her own speed. Some go back and forth between reading levels and read favorite books again and again. Others read through each level in order. You can help your young reader improve and become more confident by encouraging his or her own interests and abilities. From books your child reads with you to the first books he or she reads alone, there are I Can Read Books for every stage of reading:

SHARED READING
Basic language, word repetition, and whimsical illustrations, ideal for sharing with your emergent reader

BEGINNING READING
Short sentences, familiar words, and simple concepts for children eager to read on their own

READING WITH HELP
Engaging stories, longer sentences, and language play for developing readers

READING ALONE
Complex plots, challenging vocabulary, and high-interest topics for the independent reader

ADVANCED READING
Short paragraphs, chapters, and exciting themes for the perfect bridge to chapter books

I Can Read Books have introduced children to the joy of reading since 1957. Featuring award-winning authors and illustrators and a fabulous cast of beloved characters, I Can Read Books set the standard for beginning readers.

A lifetime of discovery begins with the magical words "I Can Read!"

Visit www.icanread.com for information
on enriching your child's reading experience.

I Can Read Book® is a trademark of HarperCollins Publishers.

Copyright © by James Dean (for the character of Pete the Cat)
Pete the Cat: Pete's Big Lunch
Copyright © 2013 by James Dean. All rights reserved. Manufactured in China. No part of this book may be used or reproduced in any manner whatsoever without written permission except in the case of brief quotations embodied in critical articles and reviews. For information address HarperCollins Children's Books, a division of HarperCollins Publishers, 10 East 53rd Street, New York, NY 10022.
www.icanread.com

Library of Congress Cataloging-in-Publication Data is available.
ISBN 978-0-06-211070-1 (trade bdg.)—ISBN 978-0-06-211069-5 (pbk.)

12 13 14 15 16 SCP 10 9 8 7 6 5 4 3 2 1 ❖ First Edition

I Can Read!

SHARED My First READING

Pete the Cat

PETE'S BIG LUNCH

created by James Dean

HARPER
An Imprint of HarperCollinsPublishers

Here comes Pete!

It is lunchtime.

Pete is ready to eat.

What should Pete eat?

A sandwich would be nice.

Yes, Pete wants a sandwich.

Pete opens the fridge.

He takes out a loaf of bread.

He finds a yummy fish.

He adds tomato and mayo.

Pete looks at his sandwich.

It is too small.

Something is missing.

Pete knows what it needs.

His sandwich needs an apple.

Pete loves apples!

His sandwich needs crackers.

Crackers are crunchy.

Pete loves crunchy crackers!

Pete looks at his sandwich again.
It is still too small.

Pete is very hungry.

Pete adds a pickle.

Pete adds cheese.

Pete adds an egg,

two hot dogs,

a banana,

and a can of beans.

Something is missing.

Pete adds ice cream!

He takes three huge scoops.

Pete's sandwich
is too big
for Pete to eat.

Pete wonders
what to do.
Pete thinks
and thinks.

"I've got it!" Pete says.
Pete calls all of his friends.

He asks them to come over.

Everyone goes to Pete's house.
They are all very hungry.

Pete shows them
his big lunch.

"Are you hungry?" asks Pete.
Pete's sandwich is big enough
for everyone.
"Dig in!" says Pete.

Pete's sandwich is good.

Pete's sandwich is VERY good.

Pete's sandwich is all gone.

Pete's friends are full.

They liked Pete's big lunch.

"Thanks for lunch,"
Pete's friends say.
"Thanks for sharing!"

"You're welcome," Pete says.
Sharing is cool.